D0435655

MINI CLASSICS

ALADDIN
AND THE
MAGIC LAMP

A PARRAGON BOOK

Published by
Parragon Books,
Unit 13-17, Avonbridge Trading Estate,
Atlantic Road, Avonmouth, Bristol BS11 9QD.

Produced by
The Templar Company plc,
Pippbrook Mill, London Road, Dorking, Surrey RH4 1JE.

Copyright © 1994 Parragon Book Service Limited

All rights reserved.

Designed by Mark Kingsley-Monks

Printed and bound in Great Britain

ISBN 1-85813-650-4

MINI CLASSICS

ALADDIN
AND THE
MAGIC LAMP

RETOLD BY STEPHANIE LASLETT
ILLUSTRATED BY HELEN COCKBURN

||| •PARRAGON• |||

O nce upon a time in far-off China there lived a poor tailor called Mustapha. He struggled hard to support his wife and his only son, Aladdin, but there was never enough money and they were often hungry. Mustapha wanted Aladdin to learn a trade and become a tailor like himself, but the boy was lazy and ran off whenever his father called.

After a time, Aladdin's idle ways made Mustapha so unhappy that he fell ill and died.

Then Aladdin grew even more
disobedient. He was never to
be found at home with his
mother but was always running
around the streets of the town
with his friends.

One day when he was playing in the streets as usual, a stranger came up and spoke to him.

"Are you the son of Mustapha the tailor?" he asked.

"I am, sir," replied Aladdin, "but he died a long while ago."

At this the stranger hugged and kissed him. "I am your uncle," he said. "I recognised you because you look just like your father. Run and tell your mother I am coming."

Aladdin ran home and told his mother the news.

"Indeed, child," she said,

"your father did have a brother, but I always thought he was dead." What she didn't know was that this was no uncle, but instead a cunning magician.

She hurried to prepare their supper, and Aladdin ran off eagerly to fetch their guest, who came laden with fruit and wine.

"Do not be surprised that we have never met before," he said to Aladdin's trusting mother, "for I have been on my travels for forty years."

He then asked Aladdin which trade he had learned. Ashamed,

the boy hung his head and his
unhappy mother burst into
tears. When the magician heard
that Aladdin was idle and would
learn no trade, he offered to
buy a shop for him and stock
it with fine goods.

Next day the magician bought Aladdin a new suit of clothes and took him all over the city, showing him the sights. He brought him home at nightfall to his mother, who was overjoyed to see her son looking so grand.

The following day the magician
took Aladdin for a walk beyond
the city gates. After a while,
they sat down by a fountain
and the magician pulled a cake
from his pocket and divided it
between them.

Then they journeyed onwards until they almost reached the mountains. Aladdin was so tired that he begged to go back, but the magician kept him amused with pleasant stories, and led him on for many more miles.

At last they came to two mountains divided by a narrow valley.

"We will go no further," said the false uncle. "Now I will show you something wonderful. Quickly gather up some sticks so I can make a fire."

When it was lit the magician took some powder from his pocket and, throwing it on the flames, muttered a strange magic spell. The earth trembled and then opened up in front of them to reveal a flat square stone with a brass ring in the middle. Aladdin was dreadfully afraid and tried to run away, but the magician caught him and gave him a blow that knocked him to the ground.

"What have I done, uncle?" he whimpered. "Don't be afraid," replied the magician more kindly, "but you must obey me. Beneath this stone lies a treasure which will be yours, and no-one else may touch it — but you must do exactly as I tell you."

At the word "treasure", Aladdin forgot his fears and did as he was bid! He grasped the ring

and heaved with all his strength.
To his astonishment, the stone
came up quite easily and he
could see steps leading down
into a dark cave.

"Go down," said the magician.
"At the foot of these steps you
will find an open door leading
into three large rooms. These
rooms lead into a garden of
fine fruit trees. Walk on until
you come to a stone wall. Look
for a hole in the wall and there
you will find a lamp. Bring it
to me carefully and we will
both be exceedingly rich."

The magician drew a ring
from his finger and gave it to
Aladdin, saying, "This will
protect you. Now go safely and
do as you have been told!"

Aladdin found everything just
as the magician had said. The
trees in the garden were laden
with strange fruit which sparkled
and gleamed in the light.

"How my mother would love
to see these," he thought, and
quickly filled his pockets to
overflowing. Soon he had
found the lamp and returned to
the mouth of the cave.

Hopping with impatience, the
magician cried out,
    "Hurry and give me the lamp!"
But Aladdin was on his guard.
He was afraid of his new uncle
and feared he might be left
underground forever.
    "No!" he cried. "First you must

help me out of the cave."

At this the magician flew into a terrible rage, for now his evil plans had been completely ruined. Some years ago, he had read in his magic books about a wonderful lamp which would make him the most powerful

man in the world. After careful study, he had worked out where it was hidden, but there was a problem. He could not fetch the lamp himself. Someone else would have to find it and bring it to him. He had picked out Aladdin for this purpose, thinking him to be a foolish good-for-nothing. He pretended to be the boy's uncle to gain his trust, but once he had the lamp, he intended to leave Aladdin in the cave forever.

Now his plot had failed and with a loud curse, the magician

threw some more powder on the fire and the stone rolled back into its place with a dreadful boom! The wicked magician fled far away to Africa, leaving Aladdin trapped in the dark cave.

For two whole days Aladdin wept bitterly. Finally, he fell on his knees and prayed to God for mercy. As he clasped his hands, he accidentally rubbed the ring which the magician had given him. With a rumble and a flash, a huge genie rose out of the ground in front of the startled Aladdin.

The boy fell flat on his face
and trembled with fear in front
of the terrifying figure.

"What is your wish?" thundered
the genie. "I am the Slave of
the Ring and will obey you in
all things."

At this, Aladdin lifted his head
and begged, "Free me from
this place!" At once the earth
opened, and he found himself
outside — but where was the
genie? Dazed and confused,
Aladdin trudged home. His
poor mother was frantic with
worry. Her son explained what

had happened, and showed her the lamp and the fruits he had gathered in the garden.

"My son, these are not fruits but precious jewels!" she cried, holding them up to the light. "But what is this old thing?" and she picked up the lamp. "Maybe if it was clean we could sell it," she said and began polishing it.

Flash! An enormous genie appeared and bowed low. Aladdin's mother fainted with surprise, but Aladdin quickly snatched the lamp and said boldly:

"Fetch me something to eat!"

Soon the genie returned. He carried twelve silver plates piled high with rich food and on his head he balanced two silver cups of wine.

And so they feasted while Aladdin told his mother about the lamp. She begged him to sell it, and have nothing to do with the genie. "No," said Aladdin. "Good luck has given this magic lamp and ring to me and I am not afraid to use them."

From then on, Aladdin sold the silver plates one by one, until he had spent all the money they fetched. Then he summoned the genie once again, requested another set of plates, and thus they lived for many months.

Now the king of this country was a mighty Sultan, rich and powerful. He had a beautiful daughter who loved to bathe in the springs of a garden nearby. The Sultan had ordered that on these days everyone was to stay home and close their shutters for it was forbidden to look at the Princess as she passed by. But Aladdin was filled with a desire to see her face.

He hid himself behind the
garden door and peeped
through a chink. The Princess
lifted her veil as she went
inside and looked so beautiful
that Aladdin fell in love with
her at first sight.

He went home and told his mother that he loved the Princess so deeply that he could not live without her, and meant to ask the Sultan, her father, for her hand in marriage. His mother burst out laughing. "The Princess would never marry *you*!" she said. "She will want to marry a Prince!"

But at last Aladdin persuaded her to visit the Sultan with his request. Then his mother remembered the magic fruits. "I will take these as a gift to the Sultan," she decided, wrapping them in a cloth. The poor woman was nervous as she entered the great hall of the palace. Seated at the far end was the Sultan, with his chief minister, the Grand Vizir, and all his lords and courtiers. Many loyal subjects had come to speak to the Sultan and the old woman had to wait her turn. At last, she found herself kneeling before him.

"Forgive me, your Majesty," she begged, "for I come with an impudent request. Aladdin, my son, has fallen in love with your daughter and wishes to marry

her. In vain have I prayed that
he might forget her. Now I
have done as he asked and beg
forgiveness, both for my son
and myself." Slowly, she unfolded
the cloth and there lay the
jewels in all their beauty.

The Sultan was thunderstruck.
He turned to the Grand Vizir
and said,

"Surely this young man
deserves the Princess if he
values her at such a high price."

But the Grand Vizir was most
displeased. He wanted the
Princess to marry his own son.

He begged the Sultan to wait for three months, hoping that in this time his son would be able to find a richer present. The Sultan agreed and told Aladdin's mother that although he gave permission for the marriage, she must now wait for three months. Aladdin was overjoyed to hear the news and waited patiently.

After two months had passed, his mother went into the city one day to buy cooking oil and found everyone rejoicing. She asked what was going on.

"Haven't you heard?" was the answer. "The son of the Grand Vizir is to marry the Sultan's daughter tonight."

Breathlessly, she ran and told Aladdin, who at first was overwhelmed with grief. But then he thought of the lamp. He rubbed it, and the genie appeared, saying, "What is your will?"

Aladdin replied, "The Sultan has broken his promise to me, and the Grand Vizir's son is to marry the princess. I command you to bring both of them here to me tonight, before the wedding."

"Master, I obey," said the genie,
and that night he returned
with the terrified Princess and
her husband-to-be.

"Lock up this man," ordered
Aladdin, pointing to the Grand
Vizir's son. As soon as he was
alone with the Princess he
spoke gently.

"Fear not, dear Princess. I only wish to save you from a marriage that should not be. Your father promised you to me if I could wait three months."

But the Princess was too frightened to speak, and passed the most miserable night of her life. In the morning, the genie fetched the shivering prisoner and carried him and the Princess back to the Palace.

Soon the Sultan and his wife came to wish their daughter good morning. But the Princess trembled and shook and would not say a word. Her father grew angry and demanded to hear the truth so at last the Princess sighed deeply and told them all that had happened the night before.

The miserable son of the Grand Vizir also admitted the truth.

"I dearly love the Princess," he added, "but I would rather die than go through another such fearful night. Break off the marriage, I beg you!"

And so the wedding was cancelled, and all the feasting and rejoicing came to an end.

Once three months had passed, Aladdin sent his mother to the palace to remind the Sultan of his promise. When he saw the old woman, the Sultan was most anxious to save his daughter from marrying into such a poor family. He turned to the Grand Vizir for advice.

"Ask Aladdin to pay such a high price for the Princess that he will never be able to afford it," whispered the crafty Grand Vizir.

And so the Sultan turned to Aladdin's mother. "Good woman,

a Sultan must remember his
promises, and I will remember
mine. But your son must first
send me forty basins of gold,
brimful with jewels, carried
by forty slaves. And all of them
must be splendidly dressed.
Tell him that I await his answer."

With that, Aladdin's mother
bowed low and went home,
thinking all was lost.

But Aladdin summoned the
genie, and in a few moments the
forty slaves arrived, and filled
the small house and garden to
overflowing.

The magnificent procession
entered the palace, led by
Aladdin's mother. The slaves
bowed low before the Sultan, and
delivered their gifts at his feet.

The Sultan was lost for words
at the sight of such splendour.
When at last he could speak,
he turned to the old woman.

"Good woman, return and tell
your son that I wait for him with
open arms." Soon Aladdin was
busy preparing for the wedding.
With a quick polish of the
lamp, he called for the genie.

"I want some fine silk clothes,

a magnificent horse and ten thousand pieces of gold in ten purses."

No sooner had he said it, than it was done. Aladdin looked so handsome that even his own mother had some difficulty recognising him.

"Now we must build a palace
fit for the Princess," he said to
the genie. "Build it of the
finest marble, set with jasper,
agate, and other precious
stones. In the middle, build me
a large hall with walls of gold
and silver. Around each window
I want a border of diamonds,
rubies and emeralds. There
shall be fine stables for my
horses and a magnificent garden
with crystal-clear fountains
and sweet-smelling flowers for
my dear Princess. Go and see
to it at once!"

Aladdin's splendid new palace was finished the next day, and everyone was astounded by its magnificence. Soon it was time for the wedding. Loud cheers filled the air as Aladdin and his mother arrived at the Sultan's Palace.

Cymbals clashed and a fanfare of trumpets rang out as the Sultan came out on to the steps to welcome them both. The Princess was well pleased by the sight of the handsome Aladdin and that night she said good-bye to her father, and set out for her new home.

"Princess," said Aladdin, "you have only your beauty to blame if my boldness displeases you."

But the Princess was far from angry. She was happy to obey her father and so the marriage took place with much rejoicing and merriment.

Aladdin's gentle nature soon won the hearts of the people. He was made Captain of the Sultan's armies, and won several battles for him, but the Grand Vizir remained suspicious, believing in his heart of hearts that Aladdin was a magician.

And so Aladdin and his Princess lived in peace and contentment for several years.

But far away in Africa the magician was brooding about the magic lamp. By his magic arts, he discovered that Aladdin, instead of perishing miserably in the cave, had escaped, and had married a Princess with whom he was living in great honour and wealth. He knew that the poor tailor's son could only have accomplished this with the help of the lamp, so he travelled night and day until he

reached the capital of China,
determined to bring about
Aladdin's ruin. As he passed
through the town he heard
people talking about a marvellous
palace with gilded walls and
jewelled windows.

"Forgive my ignorance," he asked them, "but what is this palace you speak of?"

"Have you not heard of Prince Aladdin's palace?" was the reply. "It is the greatest wonder of the world!"

Soon the magician had found the palace and straightaway guessed what had happened.

"That lamp will be mine!" he fumed, half-mad with rage, "and once again Aladdin shall live in deepest poverty."

The magician schemed and plotted and bided his time. Soon his chance came. Aladdin was leaving on a hunting trip and would be away all day. The magician bought a dozen copper lamps, put them into a basket, and hurried to the palace gates. "I will give new lamps for old!" he cried and it was such a strange offer that a jeering crowd soon followed him.

The Princess was curious and sent her servant to find out what the noise was about.

"Madam," she said, "outside there is an old fool offering to exchange fine new lamps for old ones."

The Princess laughed also and catching sight of the magic lamp on the high shelf, and knowing nothing of its power, said, "Why, there is an old lamp. Take that and fetch me a new one."

The magician nearly shouted for joy when he saw that his plan had worked. Quickly he snatched the magic lamp and, thrusting his basket at the puzzled servant girl, hurried out of the city gates to a remote hillside, where he remained until nightfall. Then he pulled out the lamp and rubbed it. With a flash, the genie appeared.

"Your wish is my command, oh, master," he said, bowing low. Clapping his hands with glee, the magician ordered the genie to carry him, together with the palace and the Princess, back to his home in Africa.

Next morning the Sultan looked out of the window towards Aladdin's palace and rubbed his eyes, for it was gone! He sent for the Grand Vizir, and he, too, was astonished.

"But I have long feared something such as this," he told the Sultan. "I believe Aladdin is a magician and has cast this spell on the Princess."

The Sultan sent thirty men on horseback to capture Aladdin. They met him riding home from the hunt. Quickly they bound him in chains and forced him to go with them on foot. But the townspeople loved Aladdin and were determined to see that he came to no harm. They followed behind, carrying swords and cudgels. Aladdin was carried before the Sultan, who ordered the executioner to cut off his head. The executioner

made Aladdin kneel down,
blindfolded him, then raised his
huge, curved scimitar in the air.
  But at that very moment the
Grand Vizir saw that the crowd
had forced their way into the
courtyard and were scaling the

walls to rescue their favourite
Prince. The Sultan could see that
his people would never forgive
him if he went ahead with the
execution so he ordered the
executioner to put down his
sword and Aladdin was unbound.

Still the crowd looked
threatening so in a loud voice
the Sultan announced that
Aladdin would be granted a
Royal Pardon. His life was safe.

Aladdin now begged to know
what he had done.

"You wretched trickster!" said
the Sultan. "Come over here,"
and he pointed to the empty
space where his palace had
once stood.

Aladdin was so amazed to see that his palace was gone that he was completely lost for words.

"Where is my daughter?" demanded the enraged Sultan. "I can accept the loss of the palace, but you must find my beloved daughter or you will lose your head."

Aladdin fell to his knees.

"The Princess means more to me than life itself," he cried. "Give me forty days and I will find her. If I should fail, then I will return and suffer my punishment."

For the next few days Aladdin
wandered about like a madman.
He had lost everything — his
palace, his Princess and his
magic lamp.

"What am I to do?" he wailed
as he tramped the streets of the
town. He asked everyone he met
if they knew what had become
of his palace, but they only
laughed and felt sorry for him.

He came to the banks of a
river and, feeling quite desperate,
decided to throw himself in
and end his sorrows. But as he
clasped his hands to say his last
prayers, he rubbed the magic
ring he still wore on his finger.

Instantly, the genie appeared.
"What is your wish, oh, master?"
he boomed.

"Save my life, genie," said Aladdin, "and bring my palace back from wherever it has gone."

"That is not in my power," said the genie. "I am only the Slave of the Ring — you must ask the Genie of the Lamp."

"Very well," said Aladdin, "Take me to the palace instead, and set me down under my dear wife's window."

No sooner had he said this than he found himself in Africa, under the window of the Princess where he fell asleep out of sheer exhaustion.

He was awakened by the singing of the birds, and for some time sat wondering what to do. He realised that all his bad luck was due to the loss of the lamp, and tried in vain to think who could have stolen it.

That morning the Princess rose early. As she dressed, she listened to the birdsong outside her window.

"How I wish I was as free as a bird," she said. "I should fly like an arrow to my dear Aladdin and leave this wretched place forever."

The magician would not let her out of the palace. Each day he visited her room and with honeyed words would try to win her love. She dreaded his knock at the door and would have forbidden him enter if she could.

With a deep sigh the Princess sat down and her maid began to brush her long hair. Suddenly the maid stopped. She had seen someone hiding outside. Quickly the Princess ran to the window and opened it wide. There stood Aladdin, and great was their joy at seeing each other again.

After they had kissed, Aladdin said, "Dear Princess, before we speak of anything else, you must quickly tell me what has become of the old lamp I left on a high shelf in the hall of our palace!"

"Alas!" she said. "It was me who caused all our sorrows for I did not know the lamp was a magic lamp. An old man came to the palace, calling 'New lamps for old!' I spied your dusty old lamp lying on the shelf and thought we had no further use for it. My maid took it outside and when she returned with a nice, new lamp I was well pleased. Oh, forgive me, Aladdin, forgive me!"

Then Aladdin understood all that happened. The Genie of the Lamp had a new master.

"Now I know who is really to blame!" cried Aladdin. "That old man was the evil magician! Quick, tell me! Where is the lamp?"

"He carries it with him all the time," said the Princess. "Once he pulled it out of his robe and showed it to me. He told me that you were beheaded on my father's orders and now he wants me to marry him. He is for ever speaking ill of you, but I can only reply with my tears."

Aladdin comforted her, and then left her for a while.

He thought long and hard and finally devised a clever plan. He visited the apothecary and bought a special powder, then returned to the Princess who let him in by a little side door.

"Put on your most beautiful dress," he told her, "and receive the magician with smiles. Make him believe that you have forgotten me. Invite him to dine with you, and say you wish to taste the wine of his country. He will go to fetch some, and while he is gone this is what you must do."

She listened carefully to Aladdin"s
plan and, after he had gone,
she dressed herself in her finery
for the first time since she left
China. She put on a necklace
and head-dress of diamonds
and as she looked in her

mirror she could see that she looked more beautiful than ever. Then she invited the magician to visit and soon he arrived at her door. She welcomed him inside with smiles and sweet words.

"I have made up my mind that Aladdin is dead, and that all my tears will not bring him back," she explained to the astonished magician. "I will mourn no more, and have therefore invited you to dine with me. But I am tired of the wines of China, and would like to taste those of Africa."

The magician bowed low to
the Princess, then hurried down
to the cellar to select the
finest of African wines. While
he was gone, the Princess put
her hand in her pocket and
pulled out the powder which
Aladdin had given her.

Quickly she poured it into
her cup. When the magician
returned, he served the wine.
The Princess asked him to
drink her health, and handed
him her cup in exchange for
his as a sign of friendship.

Before the toast, the
magician made a speech in
praise of her beauty, but the
Princess cut him short, saying
"Let us drink first, and you
shall say what you will
afterwards." She held her cup
to her lips and watched as the
magician lifted his wine and

swallowed every last drop. Slowly his eyes widened in horror and he clutched at his throat. "I have been poisoned!" he gasped and with a loud groan the magician fell lifeless to the floor.

Crying with relief, the Princess opened the door to Aladdin, and flung her arms around his neck. Then Aladdin went to the dead magician, took the lamp out of his robe and commanded the genie to carry the palace and all inside back to China once again.

The Sultan sat all alone in his
room, mourning his lost
daughter. For the hundredth
time that day he looked out of
the window to the spot where
Aladdin's palace used to be.
Suddenly he jumped to his feet
and rubbed his eyes, for there
stood the palace, exactly the
same as before!

The Sultan ran up the marble
steps and was overjoyed to
find his precious daughter safe
and well. Angrily, he turned to
Aladdin and demanded to hear
the truth.

"My story is true, for I could never trick your Majesty," said Aladdin. "This evil magician spirited away your daughter but now he is dead and we can all live in peace ever more."

The Sultan was so delighted by their return that he ordered

of ten days feasting and after this Aladdin and his wife did indeed live in peace in their beautiful palace. When the Sultan died, Aladdin took his place and reigned for many years, leaving behind him a long line of just and beloved kings.

Aladdin belongs to one of the greatest story collections of all time: *The Tales of the Arabian Nights*. These stories were first heard many hundreds of years ago and include *The Voyages of Sinbad the Sailor* and *The Magic Carpet*.

First translated into French by Antoine Galland at the beginning of the 18th century, they were originally told by the beautiful Princess Scheherezade to the suspicious Prince of Tartary, who had threatened to behead her at daybreak. But her tales were so exciting that, as the sun rose, he longed to hear how they ended and so pardoned her life for one more day, until after one thousand and one nights Scheherezade had won his trust and his heart.